I0766078

Published in the first edition in 2025 by:
CJ Waterfield
Carranwaterfield.co.uk
Carran@carranwaterfield.co.uk

ISBN
Hardback: 978-1-7397469-3-3

Pink Granite

A tale about roots, stone and a book

In memory of my late friend Fiona Elizabeth Fearnhead
(1957–2022)

Carran Waterfield

Illustrated by Fruzsina Czech

Contents

Pink Granite

Prologue

Have you heard of Brinepoint, the city by the sea situated on the long peninsula where everyone lives on the same level? If you have, you will know of Redhair and Daffodil Friend, best-friend sisters and the daughters of Sea Potato Mam, Governor of Brinepoint. You will also know how the girls learned what a challenge it can be when your mam leaves you in charge … of everything while she goes off to work – in their case for nine whole years!

***

'Don't go poking about in other people's business. You may regret it,' Sea Potato Mam warned her daughters, now young women. They had been driving her mad with questions about who was related to whom. Why did people have the same first name as their surname? Why weren't some nick-pet-names recorded? Why did some people born in Brinepoint have ancestors who were born in a place called Core Rock? What was the meaning of the umbrella stamp on some of the certification? Was it something to do with the time before the magic needle? Who were the One Ears of Brinepoint? Were they also the One Ears of Core Rock?

Sea Potato Mam wasn't keen on looking back. If anything, she thought mainly about the future, always dreaming of an invention to provide a solution to Brinepoint's continuing weather problems. Currently she was working on forest fires and rising sea levels. There had to be a way for the fires to be extinguished effectively using seawater through magnetic forces, she mused. She was considering a flying hose that would swallow up large quantities of seawater and spew it out at the sound of the first siren.

Science and engineering were of little interest to Redhair and Daffodil Friend these days. They still believed in magic and books containing strange instructions. Between you and me, of course, we know they boil down to the same thing. Now eighteen years old, the young women daily poked about in the city hall where the lists of all the newborns were kept. You could trace the Brinepoint families through the colour schemes. To know their own heritage had become the women's sole mission.

'People are just as important as the inventions they come up with,' they argued. 'We need to know our roots. We need to know where we come from.' Sea Potato Mam pored over her drawings.

'Well, I wasn't born under a gooseberry bush, and if you won't explain to me who my dad is, I'll have to find out myself.'

'And if no one knows anything about either of mine, I'm doing the same as Redhair,' quipped Daffodil Friend, now nick-pet-named Daff for short. She believed her real family had come from far away. She knew she was left on the steps of the city hall as a baby, adopted by Sea Potato Mam and then slept for six years during the dark smoky time when One Ear took over. But she found it hard to believe anything she was told about those six long years. It sounded so terrifying.

The young women spent hours in the city hall poring over registration documents, scrutinising the most indecipherable handwriting they had ever seen as they tried to make sense of dates and place names, new names for old names and the occasional nick-pet-name for an original one sewn by the magic key under their mam's governance and invention.

Today, the city's chief archivist had given them special permission to look at the untouchables in the great vault under the city chamber. There was everything to look forward to.

'Be careful what you wish for,' Sea Potato Mam called to them as they rushed out of the house, where they lived still adjacent to the tower mechanism operated by the magic key. The door clattered shut behind them. The tower mechanism dutifully chugged away, sweetening the city's water, the way it always did.

***

'When you look out to sea from the top of one of the three mountains that existed before Brinepoint came about, you will see an island. When the tide is out, it looks like the island is joined to the mainland. When the tide is in, the island looks like it is its very own kingdom. From high above, if you fly like a bird, you will see the island has the shape of a fairy's or an elf's head, depending on the way you look at the world. But whichever way you look, you can tell by the ears and the chin. It's the place of the One Ears.'

The city archivist was reading from a very old local history book that described the historical and geological nature of Brinepoint in 'rather a poetically geological and historical way', said the archivist, who continued reading to the insatiable young women who hung on every word.

'Before Brinepoint was named thus, it was called Core Rock. It was a place where digging was the main activity of the people who lived there. Quarrying, another name for digging, can be a soft activity if the earth is soft. But in Core Rock, the earth is, as the name implies, made of rock, so in Core Rock we call it quarrying. At the time of writing, the quarrying is happening out of the second mountain. Each quarried-out mountain – and there are two at the time of writing – looks just like an ear. The quarry spirals into the centre to a point you could almost whisper into – that is, if you are a bird flying above and swooping down, as the ravens do around this place. At the time of writing there is much activity going on in the village of Core Rock. We have come to this place at a very important time indeed.'

The young women were shaking with excitement. Already here was a clue to their questions about the birth of Brinepoint before the city was named thus.

'Now, I have brought you another book to look at. This one is very precious, so be careful as you turn the pages. I will place it on a cushion for you. You must wear soft white gloves, and you can only use pencil if you are making notes,' said the Chief Archivist, taking both young women through *Rules for Researching Your Family History*, an instruction book that sat alongside the rulebook *On the Care of Lost Children*, which Daff had already read several times in case it held a clue about her own story.

Family history research was not a popular activity in Brinepoint, because research like this was considered interfering in other people's business, which was frowned upon. Nevertheless, our young researchers needed some answers. So they opened the first page of the book. They read the following instruction etched onto the parchment:

'Lick your finger, close your eyes and let it fall on the page at a precise word.'

How could they do that with the gloves on?

Chapter One
Teatime

Pink Granite

'There was once a very old umbrella that stuck out of the top of a mountain like a chimney sweep's brush.'

Great Great Old Granny Pink was telling one of her ancient tales to Sarah and Ella One Ear. She did this every year when the hacking and cracking and tapping stopped in the mountain and the lads came home for their tea.

'How do you spell umbrella?' asked Sarah, always curious for the facts. 'Is it um-ber-ella like under the brella like our Ella? Or is it umbrella like umbrage, like when our Will gets very cross and confused and his head is banging with the hammers? I mean like umbrage like when you're storming about something. I mean downright stark raving mad about something. I mean VOLCANIC!'

The clouds crashed and lightning flashed through the windows like it would split the cottage in two. Hitting the fireplace, it made the plates clatter and quake on the mantelshelf. Ella flew towards the fire to catch them. It wasn't necessary, but she always did things like that. She was often thinking ahead, recognising a catastrophe that could happen. Ella worried a lot.

The girls chanted while Great Great Old Granny Pink rocked hard in her chair, the thud of the rockers accompanying their spell.

'Umberella
Umbragella
Umber
Umber
Uber
Umber
Über
Under
Over
Downhill
Down-about-it
All-about-it
All-in-a-thingama-bob-bob-bob

Pink Granite

Bbb-blobbing
Blinking
Blanking
Blonking
Blank blot
On the landscape
That big blank blot on the landscape
Who owns that blinking big black blot
Of an excuse of a thingamabob that pokes up
Like that?!'

The girls fell about laughing. Great Great Old Granny Pink had rocked herself so hard that her petticoats had flown over her head, revealing her pink knickerbockers in all their glory.

The latch of the cottage door lifted and in walked Great Old White Beard One Ear in a cloud of dust. He scraped his boots hard on the doormat, hacking and clacking and clearing his crackling chest like he always did when he got home from work. He spat in the sink, took a pot of water and swished the spit away.

'Have you got the tea on, Mam?'

Ella and Sarah One Ear flicked Granny's skirts back over her lap. They held to steadfast attention their laughter, for fear of a clip round the ear.

Great Great Old Granny Pink cocked her head in the direction of the stove, while Ella and Sarah obediently pulleyed the pot down into its place to heat over the fire.

The latch of the cottage door lifted and in walked Old Brother Stone Face One Ear in a cloud of dust. He scraped his boots hard on the doormat, hacking and clacking and clearing his crackling chest like he always did when he got home from work. He spat in the sink, took a pot of water and swished the spit away.

'Have you got the tea on, Mam?'

'Yes, we've got the tea on,' chorused the girls.

Great Great Old Granny Pink cocked her head in the direction of the larder, where the milk from their cow was already prepared in a blue-and-white-striped jug.

'One two three, time for tea,' they recited, carefully carrying the milk jug to the table for the men of the house returning from the quarry.

The latch of the cottage door lifted and in walked Brother Will One Ear in a cloud of dust. He scraped his boots hard on the doormat, hacking and clacking and clearing his crackling chest like he always did when he got home from work. He spat in the sink, took a pot of water and swished the spit away.

'Have you got the tea on, Mam?'

'Yes, we've got the tea on,' chorused the girls.

Great Great Old Granny Pink cocked her head in the direction of the blue-and-white-striped mugs hanging within the dresser.

'One two three, time for tea,' chanted the sisters as they counted out the mugs for the men of the house.

It happened like this every day, six days a week when the men returned from the mountain, unless it was a holiday or a funeral or a wedding or a naming. Every day, Ella and Sarah One Ear served tea and oat cakes to their grandfather and their brothers while Great Great Old Granny Pink rocked in her chair, singing songs about heaven and bread and all the suffering ever dreamed of. On the seventh day they all went to the blessing hut, like they did for a funeral or a wedding or a holiday or if there was a special meeting called.

But today it was different. Today the men would not be going back to the quarry. Today they would be staying home for three whole years. It was the striking time. It was the angry time.

Pink Granite

They were strong.
They were old.
They were clever.
They were great,
the old ones,
those old men of the hills.

They were their hills.
They worked them,
searched them,
lived in them,
them quarrymen.

Angry men.
Danger men.
Edgy men.
Tough men.
Rough men.
Hard men.

Men who counted,
Men who measured,
Men who cut,
Men who scraped,
Men who bent,
while their mothers baked batches of bread.

Chapter Two
The Stone Baby

Pink Granite

The men had gone to a meeting at the Green Circle. All the men from Core Rock were attending. Ella and Sarah One Ear had little to do until they came back. They had finished all their chores: all the sewing and the knitting and the washing and the milking and the sloshing and the slashing and the cutting and the scraping.

'Tell us the one about the baby of stone,' urged the sisters, their hands clutching and rustling at Great Great Old Granny Pink's skirts.

The old woman seemed almost asleep, but her eyes were wide open. She was in a trance. The girls giggled excitedly. This was going to be a good version, they thought, for they had heard this story many times.

Great Great Old Granny Pink began to rock and then she spoke.

'I am going through the passing place where she walked along the edge.'

The girls writhed with excitement, wondering who she was, for this was a new bit.

'I see a green sea remembering, re-membering, dismembering me.'

The girls shuddered. Was she going to die? Was she going to join the union with the men? What did she mean? Was she going to be cut up and put in a pot? Should they get help next door?

Great Great Old Granny Pink snapped out of it and came to. She dutifully went into the story they had asked for.

'Once upon a time there was a woman who gave birth to a stone – not an ordinary stone,
a special one.
For nine months she carried that stone over land and sea until she came to the edge of the world where there grew a tree anchored by its roots in the heart of the sea.
Suddenly the tree spoke to the woman.

"I am your sister-mother, and she is my child in whom I am well pleased.
I have brought you to this place so that you might give me back my child."

Pink Granite

The woman could not believe that such a miracle could be taken away from her so
soon.
Her tears filled the ocean
till she felt that she would almost drown
in the sorrow of her
sister-mother.'

Great Great Old Granny Pink ceased her storytelling for a moment, for she saw
something.

'She can see the funnel and the crown again, Ella,' said Sarah.

'The earth, the earth needs to breathe,' wailed the old woman. 'I am suffocating.'

The girls wrapped their arms around their granny with assuring pats. Ella took up the
story, for she wanted to say it and she wanted to tell it and she wanted to know if she
knew it all off by heart by now.

Ella spoke in hushed tones, taking up her great-granny's story.

'So the tree-mother relented upon one condition:
"You must make a coat out of my bark,
out of my blossoms,
out of my leaves,
out of my apple skins,
so that my child may be comfortable in all weathers.

Then, once a year you must return to this place with the child.
Put the coat on the child.
Put the child at my roots,
In the heart of my roots,
so I may hold her close." '

Then Great Great Old Granny Pink, recovering from her reverie, took up the story,
rocking as she did with a thud and a creak on the slate floor of the kitchen where

she sat every day minding her great-granddaughters, whose mother had been lost to them during the coughing time.

'She placed the child on the seashore for safekeeping.
And then, taking a deep breath, she cast herself into the sea.'

The girls loved this part of the story and chanted along together:

'At the end of the first season,
she surged to the surface of the water
to collect the leaves of the tree.
At the end of the second season,
she surged to the surface of the water
to collect the fruits of the tree.
At the end of the third season,
she surged to the surface of the water
to collect the bark of the tree.
At the end of the fourth season,
she surged to the surface of the water
to collect
to collect the petals of the tree
in all their budded jades and frosted rose blossoms.'

They gasped for breath from the story and the long chant. All three were entranced by the tale and chorused together like the end of an anthem from the Lord's Steeple House or a wild visiting preacher bent on increasing his conversions:

'By the end of the fourth season she had woven the coat.'

The latch of the cottage door lifted and in walked Great Old White Beard, Old Brother Stone Face and Brother Wild Will in their smart Sunday best. They placed their hats on metal hooks on the back of the door and scraped their boots hard on the doormat. They weren't coughing today, for they had not been to the quarry.

The dust had settled and the mountain was silent.

The quarry was quiet and still, as it had been for a year now.

'Have you got the tea on, Mam?' they chorused.

'Yes, we've got the tea on,' responded the girls.

Great Great Old Granny Pink One Ear cocked her head in the direction of the stove, the larder and the dresser, where everything was already prepared for coming home from the meeting.

'One two three, time for tea,' they recited, carefully placing the kettle on the stove, carrying the milk jug to the table and the blue-and-white-striped mugs from the dresser for the men returning home from the meeting.

The girls wondered if there was news. The hushed whispers from the men suggested it was still the angry time. The men finished their tea, picked up their hats and left the house.

'No news, then,' said Great Great Old Granny Pink and concluded her story for the girls.

'She placed the garment on the child, gave thanks and,
with the child, cast herself into the sea,
down to the heart of the tree-mother
where her roots were anchored.
And there they rested.
And to this day the woman and her stone baby have never returned.'

Then the girls and the old woman sang the song of the Great Lamentation, one often sung at funerals held in the blessing hut:

'Lalayo lalayo lalayo layo layo
Lalayo lalayo lalayo layo layo
Lalayo lalayo lalayo layo layo
Lalayo lalayo lalayo layo layo.'

Chapter Three
The Blessing Hut

Pink Granite

One day a week, the resting day, everyone went to what we might call church or mosque or temple and so on. In the quarry village there was no calling or bells chiming to remind people to go. Instead, the eldest child in each family popped their head out of their doorway every fifteen seconds from the first cock crowing to check if Great Great Old Granny Pink had stepped onto her cottage doorstep to make the journey up the stony pathway to the blessing hut.

'Has she gone yet?'

'No, she hasn't.'

The stony pathway was still and silent.

'Yes, she has!'

Great Great Old Granny Pink's laced-up black-booted foot peeked out of the door.

'No, she hasn't.'

Her boot had popped back in again.

'Yes, she has!'

Two boots were peeking over the threshold.

'No, she hasn't.'

They'd gone turnaround back in again.

This same chorus happened in each household up and down the lane every resting day, the eldest child in each family keeping watch. It was tradition.

'Yes, she has!'

The hat – she'd put on that hat, the enormous mountain-shaped hat that almost flattened her tiny body. Great Great Old Granny Pink strutted, book in hand, up the stony pathway to the blessing hut. Great Old White Beard, Old Brother Stone Face, Brother Will, Ella and Sarah One Ear followed dutifully behind. And every Sunday the entire lane followed her in line. The eldest family member held a book in their hand, each family filing up the stony pathway to the blessing hut.

The blessing hut was a smallish oblong building with a point at each end, not like a roof with two points but like a small turret at each end that was round but pointed on top. There was only one entrance, and the entrance was the exit. There was no back door. Before you went in through the wooden door you had to knock on the knocker and say, 'Is there anybody there?' And the person that went in before you had to say, 'Yes, and that person be you, kind friend.' Then you would step inside and become the guardian of the door. You had to wait for the next person to knock and you would answer in turn to the next person and so on. Everything was taken in turns. It was tradition. It was always best to get there first, because then you would be the one to whom Great Great Old Granny Pink would say, 'Yes, and that person be you, kind friend.' And that always felt special. By the time people had got to the door there would be a lot of pushing and shoving, overtaking and undercutting. It's understandable in a place like Core Rock, because the people didn't have much. People thought that the nearer they could get to Great Great Old Granny Pink One Ear, the closer they would be to fortune and passage from this place of hard toil. For it was hard toil, especially now, during the angry time.

Life was so hard in Core Rock that many had left in search of work elsewhere and many had gone to fight in the wars in faraway places, as you will hear of later. But many stayed and kept their hope that things would change for the better once they had made their case to the Lord, the One Ears being one of those families.

Once inside the blessing hut, there sat Great Great Old Granny Pink One Ear in her blessing hut rocking chair, book open, about to read the blessing. People sat around her on benches, heads bowed. They mumbled low mutterings which grew louder and stronger, like the rumbling you get after an explosion in the quarry.

Pink Granite

'O bless me, ye One Ears of the Ancient Times.
Ye are my solace, ye One Ears of the Ancient Times,
My rock and fortune, ye One Ears of the Ancient Times.
Bring me sustenance, ye One Ears of the Ancient Times.'

 And then everyone began to mutter in their own made-up languages with a freedom of expression not to be heard anywhere else on earth, I think.

Then the singing came. If you believe in angels, it was angels who sang through the hearts of the believers in the One Ears of the Ancient Times.

After about fifteen minutes, the singing hushed and Great Great Old Granny Pink flicked through her book. She nodded to Ella, her assistant this week. Ella approached the rocking chair, her finger leading the way. Then she licked her leading index finger, closed her eyes, and let it fall on the page at a precise word. The word was 'Jimmy'.

'Jimmy's story,' revealed Great Great Old Granny Pink.

'Jimmy's story, Jimmy's story, Jimmy's story,' chanted the gathering.

Reading from the book, it went:

'One day,
Running down that hill,
The grey one came,
His fingers flapping,
His jacket snapping
In the mountain wind that had tossed
His locks all over the shop.

"Disaster! Disaster!
Jimmy's fell off the edge," he called.
"Ring the bell,
Fetch the stretcher.
He's hurt real bad.
Get his mother!"

Pink Granite

The Grand Old Duke had gashed his shin
And ripped his ear off
Marching up and down that hill.
Up Up
Down Down
Ten thousand of them quarrymen
In a dispute over health and safety.

When Jimmy went over the edge
His pouch went with him.
The gravel went with him.
His snap went with him.
His wages went with him.
And he left his ear halfway up and halfway down.

When a tree with a sticky out leg
Ripped into his shin,
His heart stopped beating for five whole minutes.
In those five whole minutes,
Jimmy had a vision.

He saw a woman in black
With a stick,
A pot and a spoon.
And he saw himself
Standing on a throne,

His head popping out of a cushion at the top of a mountain.

Gash Gash Gash!
Gosh Gosh Gosh!'

At the end of the old, old story, Sarah and Ella went to the part of the hut where the tea mugs hung, in the far turret end, and began to prepare hot tea and oat cakes for the flock of followers.

The hungry and thirsty hands of the quarriers and their families clutched the mugs and oat cakes with gratitude as they shared stories of their labours and their leisure. This went on until twelve noon, then everyone tottered off to their cottages for ham and cheese sandwiches that Ella and Sarah had packed up for them ready to take away. The sandwiches were made with the bread the mothers had baked, along with the ham and cheese they had purchased for a florin from the Grand Old Lord's Charity for Farmers. The last left first, and the first left last. Then Great Great Old Granny Pink put on her hat, locked the door of the blessing hut and followed her family home down the stony path.

Chapter Four
It Is the Lord's Time

Ella had finished her work and was poking about in the drawers in the dresser where Great Great Old Granny Pink kept her book. Sarah was sat at the windowsill with piles of socks that needed to be darned. I bet you are thinking, if you are a modern person, that this all seems a bit gender unbalanced here. How come all the boys and men are working (well, now not working) at the quarry and all the women are either sewing, baking or darning socks? Well, in those days it was like that. It was part of the way to keep people in their places. Like when you sit up straight at the table, don't speak with your mouth full and only speak when you are spoken to. It was tradition. However, if you could get to a book, much might be possible.

Great Great Old Granny Pink was snoring in the corner, her rocking chair finally still, resting from its constant banging, just like the men, who had suspended their smashing and cracking and cutting and hacking, because, as you know, it was the angry time. Ella had carefully pulled Great Great Old Granny Pink's book from the dresser drawer. It was quite heavy and old – ancient, even. It smelled like gone-off cheese from the pantry or Brother Will's socks that he'd forgotten to put in the wash basket.

She closed her eyes and held it aloft, letting it fall open at any page. Then, wetting her index finger, she placed it on a random word. Wounded Crag stuck out like a sore thumb. No, she thought. I don't want that one. That will be about Jimmy One Ear again. So she tried again. She let the book fall open at any page and, wetting her index finger, placed it on a random word. Sea Stone stuck out like a sore thumb. No, she thought. I don't want that one either. It will be about the island and the Grand Old Lord. I want something about us. I want something about Core Rock. So she tried again. She let the book fall open at any page and, wetting her index finger, placed it on a random word. This time it was more than one word. It was a title: How the Mountains Got Broken. She began to read aloud to Sarah, who was still darning away at the windowsill.

'You'll be in trouble,' warned Sarah.

Ella, ignoring her sister, began to read:

Pink Granite

'Are you wondering?
Do you know
Of that city by the sea
Near the edge
At the edge
On the edge?

Drink your tea.'

The girls slurped from their mugs of tea, which Ella had already prepared, knowing they would need tea if a ritual came up. She continued reading:

'Over the cliff edge
The cliff is crumbling
Rock
Pink rock
Like rhubarb
Like giant rhubarb leaves
Rhubarb and custard
Umbrella leaves

Drink your tea.'

The girls slurped from their mugs the tea that Ella had already prepared, knowing they would need tea if a ritual came up. She continued reading:

'Custard skin
And jug ear leaves
Seaside leaves
Ice cream milk and dairy cow leaves
Dairy farmer fishwife
Fisher
Fiskmann
Pescetarianman
Vegan Man

Pink Granite

Vegetarian
Carcass
Meat chop
Dig and cut.
Dig and cut.
Smash your cup!'

The girls, without thinking, smashed their mugs of tea on the hard stone floor. Great Great Old Granny Pink stirred and snorted but slept on. Ella continued reading:

'In the granite quarry of your grandfathers at Stoney Stanton,
Bedworth
and Coverntree,
In Richard's Red Leicester out at Broughton Astley
Blasting the ship foghorns bound for
Canada, Brownsburg and Quebec
A baby, a wife and on
Through the Great War.
Ride the Horse that is Teuton
Then come back again.'

It was a prophecy, thought Ella as she tried to make sense of the words that didn't seem to belong to their time.

There was a stirring and a grinding in the corner.

'You got hold of my book? You naughty girl rooting through my drawers behind my back!'

Ella flinched at the scolding. Sarah put her head down, stabbing her finger with the needle.

'Ouch!'

Blood oozed through the sock she was working on.

Pink Granite

Ella grabbed the broom to clear up the broken mugs.

'That'll teach you, you little b …' Almost rising to give a clip round the ear. Then Great Great Old Granny Pink thankfully dozed off again.

In Great Great Old Granny Pink's book, anyone who was present at the crime was guilty, so Sarah was also culpable and deserved the prick from heaven, as so she thought. Sarah also worried a lot, thinking long and hard on these things, trying to understand what truth was and what was fable, feeling the guilt even though she had given the warning not to read from the book.

Ella sighed with relief that the scolding had been only momentary and went back to the book.

'At the edge
Of the mountain
There's a Fairy Goblin
With a black and pink spotted Umbrella
Eating rhubarb and custard with the skin on
While Andersen and Danny's Thumbelina
Watch from the lap of a Gunnera
In Sandra's garden.
In those days they will say,

"I see a city
I see a city overlooking water
Its limbs long and thin
No land North
No land East
No land West
Flat
Flat
Flat land.
The third gone.
The second gone.

Pink Granite

The first gone.

When the master comes wearing the mountain called Sea Stone
You will be next, and you will be the last." '

Sarah and Ella stared at each other aghast. They strained to interpret the words. Grand Old Lord Sea Stone, the Lord of the Quarry – had he called the meeting? Had he caused the angry time? Was he the one the men were going to see in the Green Circle? Sea Stone, Giant Town and our village Core Rock, our mountains. Giant Town has already gone. Sea Stone built the castle on the island using the rock from Giant Town and some of Core Rock! What more does he want from Core Rock? Are we going to be last? Won't the last be first? All these questions and worries were racing around in the girls' minds.

Chapter Five
Grand Old Lord Sea Stone

Grand Old Lord Sea Stone lived every inch a Lord, fully, widely and flatly. He lorded it over the mountains. He lorded it over the sea. He lorded it over the cottages. He lorded it over the roads. He lorded it far and wide up the hill and down the dale, as far as the eye could see. Who would put up with that? you might be thinking to yourself. Well, the villagers had for many years. He owned the mountains, and they quarried the mountains. He owned their houses, and they rented their houses as part of their wages. He paid their wages, and they were grateful.

But today in the angry time, the quarrymen were saying enough is enough, or so Sarah and Ella had gleaned from the hushed tones of Brother Wild Will, Old Brother Stone Face and Great Old White Beard.

Grand Old Lord Sea Stone had built for himself a castle on the island with many corridors and spacious rooms. You could get to it by boat when the tide was in, or you could walk to it when the tide was out.

Grand Old Lord Sea Stone was the richest man ever to live, or at least that Sarah and Ella had ever known to live. The rumour was that he had made his fortune sailing the seas, bumping into land, getting the local people to work for him for nothing or just a few trinkets. He would then bring back the local bounty to use for his projects on the island. The island was his place; somewhere he went to when he wanted time to think and plan. He spent so much time thinking and planning that he built the castle to house all his plans. Sometimes he would bring the locals from faraway places back to work in the castle's spacious rooms and corridors. You might think him a selfish man. You might think him a vain man. But he gave charity where he thought charity was needed. He opened hospitals. He set up a school. He launched a Festival Fund. In fact, he oozed charity. He would throw florins out of his study window every holiday time. The women of Core Rock gratefully gathered the florins in their aprons and their skirts, stooping low as they stepped home backwards over the sand to the village, never lifting their heads out of respect for one so grand and generous, or so they thought.

Sarah had seen one of his rooms when Great Great Old Granny Pink had taken her over to clean the silver when she worked there before the angry time and before she got sleepy.

Pink Granite

The room Sarah had seen was full of paintings of the Grand Lord himself doing charitable acts. There was one of him holding the hand of a wounded quarryman on a stretcher. There was one of him knocking on a cottage door with a food parcel in winter. There was another one of him by a tree holding a spade alongside a small group of little saplings it looked like he had just planted. Then there was one of him wearing a wraparound coat of pink shimmering with ridges and lines, a replica of the quarry patterning that sparkled in the background. Grand Old Lord Sea Stone wore his charities like Joseph's Coat of Many Colours. His friends and relatives sang about him in the Steeple House, where all the rich went to pray.

> All glory, laud and honour
> To thee, redeemer King!
> To whom the lips of children
> Made sweet hosannas ring.
> Thou art the king of Egypt
> And we all know it's true.
> All glory, laud and honour
> And all's the same to you.

And all the rich children dressed in quarry children's clothes sang:

> Sea Stone bids us shine with a pure clear light,
> Like a little candle burning in the night.
> In this world of darkness we will shine,
> You in your small corner and me in mine.

Grand Old Lord Sea Stone, the Lord of the Quarry – had he called all the meetings? Was he the one the men were going to see in the Green Circle?

Ella and Sarah still worried over these questions, then Great Great Old Granny Pink stirred again from her sleep. She had forgotten the crime the two had committed and was humming a hymn from the Steeple House. Then she spoke in a trance once again:

Pink Granite

'I'm very busy this morning watering my apple tree.
And do we know why I'm watering my apple tree?
Because I'm related to the Queen.
Great Great Old Granny Pink is of royal descent. I've got the royal blood.
Great Great Old Granny Pink's blue blood
is flowing fast and furiously through this house, isn't it?

I am a Queen. I am the Queen of this house.
I run it from top to bottom.
See now that I, even I am she!
I wound and I heal. I kill and I bring back to life!

On your knees!
Bow before me and my kingdom will be your kingdom.
And my inheritance will be your inheritance.
And my children will be your children.
And MY daughters … will be your daughters
and they shall bear fruit
and the fruit shall bear fruit
and the fruit of the fruit shall bear fruit
and the fruit of the fruit of the fruit shall bear fruit
and we will create together an apple tree for the nation
The taproot of the nation!'

Ella and Sarah quivered and shook, not knowing what had overcome Great Great
Old Granny Pink, who was speaking like the people from the Steeple House, all grand
and high and mighty. It was terrifying.

She continued:

'Thou hast to get thee away to a far country,
for Thou art banish-ed.
The old man says thou art not wanted in this house.

Thou shalt not trespass on this property ever again.
Do not darken our doorstep ever again.
Thou art not wanted in this vicinity.
Take thyself hence and be gone!
They are going to the Green Circle
They are going to the meeting with the Great Lord.'

At this, Great Great Old Granny Pink collapsed on the hard stone floor and the men walked in from the meeting. That was a pretty bad thing to happen, because it was the eve of the Florin Flinging.

Chapter Six
The Bargain

Pink Granite

'What's been going on here? Fetch the Dark One,' bellowed Great Old White Beard. He feared for his mam.

The Dark One was already at the cottage door sharp on the tails of the men. She had brought her bag of oak leaves, meadowsweet and broom, with the essence of which she concocted a steaming pot to revive Great Great Old Granny Pink.

Sarah and Ella trembled with fear, the memory of their mother dying during the coughing time panging in their hearts. They dare not remind Great Old White Beard of his wife's sad passing.

'Please not Granny Pink, please not Granny Pink,' they cried inwardly.

But he was remembering. Tears trickled down his cheeks, soaking his white beard. His rage had subsided to a gentle weeping.

Outside, a clattering of boots could be heard on the stony path. The women were flocking up the path to the blessing hut for the usual speech before Florin Flinging Day. The day before Florin Flinging was a women's day. It always had been. It was tradition. The three quarrymen were caught between their knowledge from today's earlier meeting at the Green Circle and the dilemma of Granny Pink's sudden fall.

'We must tell 'em,' urged Old Brother Stone Face. 'It was agreed at the meeting. No Florin Flinging Day this year, no fraternising with the Lord until it's settled.'

Brother Will tossed his head in the direction of his ailing grandmother. 'She needs to tell 'em. She's the speaker,' he blurted out, not always the most tactful in his timing.

'Well, she's not speaking tonight!' scolded Great Old White Beard.

Chastised, Will pulled a small bottle from his pocket and took a swig. It was how he pacified himself for his mistakes. He didn't mean to be so tactless. He had learned the rules from his dad, but somehow when he put them into action, he always got it wrong. So he drank. He drank a lot, especially when he knew his dad was angry with him. What he was drinking Sarah and Ella didn't know, but it smelled juicy on his breath and always gave him a headache after he had drained the bottle dry.

The Dark One was used to the ailments in the village. She had brought at least two generations of quarry children into the world. She was the one everyone went to if something awkward came up. Ella and Sarah had taken her talking treatment after their mam had passed. It had helped – a little.

Then there was a thundering on the door.

In walked Tommy Left Foot, in a fluster. Tommy Left Foot was not from the One Ear clan. In fact, no one knew his clan, apart from his mam, and she had died when he was born. Of course, the Dark One knew, but she never spoke about it. Instead, the Dark One had taken on Tommy and brought him up as her own.

'The women, they're going berserk at the door of the blessing hut. We've got to give them the message as one. We agreed. No Florin Flinging. No fraternising with Sea Stone till it's settled. White Beard One Ear, we need you at the hut along with Old Granny Pink for the message.' Tommy Left Foot was distraught with worry.

Then he saw the scene and realised the dilemma, seeing the unconscious Granny Pink on the bed in the kitchen.

But he was stuck in his mind with an irksome image. Old Lord Sea Stone would see the women's open aprons at dawn and think they were on his side and the men would return to work. It would seem to him that a bargain had been struck. Though he wasn't a One Ear, Tommy certainly had the nous of a One Ear and was now aware of what could happen. It would be a disaster for the men. They would lose the argument if their womenfolk fraternised with the Lord.

'The tide is going out and the women are on the move. Blessing hut message or no blessing hut message, we must stop the women. We must show unity. It was agreed in the Green Circle,' insisted Tommy. His devotion to the cause and the urgency of the long and weary angry time beat in his heart and stormed his imagination. The men of the village had suffered a whole year off the mountain while the quarry was silent. It would be madness to give in to Grand Old Lord Sea Stone now, after all the suffering and the arguments and the need to get an agreement.

Neither Ella nor Sarah could make head nor tail of the ensuing conversation. Worried for Great Great Old Granny Pink and her position in the community, there was only one thing to do. During the kerfuffle, the stress and the men's agitation, they seized the book from the drawer in the dresser and left the cottage. The men were too busy with Tommy's suggestion of the strike being broken to notice the girls' disappearance and the little cottage filling up with even more worried quarrymen.

The men looked to Great Great Old Granny Pink for a swift recovery, relying on the skill of the Dark One they trusted, since they knew she had borne them, healed them and consoled them for most of their lives.

The thing is, though, these quarrymen, despite their hardness and their mettle, always melted when their mams waned. The men did odd things when the going got tough. What they might have considered women's jobs seemed to desert them. They boiled kettles, made tea, scratched their heads and wiped each other's brows in all the steam and the panic. They pondered on the dilemma, drank tea and asked for a miracle from the Dark One.

Meanwhile, at the top of the stony path and scrambling to the front of the queue at the blessing hut, Sarah and Ella addressed the gathered crowd of women.

Chapter Seven
The Message

Pink Granite

'Great Great Old Granny Pink is ailing. The Dark One is at her side. But we have got the book. All will be well. The men say there will be no Florin Flinging this year. We must keep an agreement. We must stand together. No fraternising with Lord Sea Stone. We must go without the florins.'

There was uproar!

'Who do you think you are?'

'Who put you in charge?'

'What on earth are you talking about?'

'It's tradition. We've always done it.'

'You can't stop the Florin Flinging!'

'You couple of upstarts!'

'Where is Granny Pink?'

'Where is Granny Pink?'

'Where is Granny Pink?' they cried.

'We are Granny Pink,' shrieked Ella and Sarah above the din. 'We are her representatives. We know how it goes. We've got the book and we know the ritual.'

Terrified of the crowd of women but so well versed in the ways of the blessing hut, taught them by their granny, they held their own and opened the door.

Standing in the doorway, 'We will ask the stone,' they called.

The crowd suddenly hushed. If ever the stone was to be asked, there was nothing to be said about it. You just had to listen.

The stone was their livelihood. It had been for years. You respected the stone. You loved the stone. You served the stone. Everyone in the village knew that. So, following the routine known to them all, they knocked on the door in the ritual fashion until each and every woman was inside, along with their children. It was getting dark by the time the last woman and child had entered the blessing hut. The tide was almost out between the island and the mainland. The castle was in clear view.

A crowd of men gathered in the Green Circle, which was near the second turret of the blessing hut. They had had arguments with their wives earlier that day about the Florin Flinging after they had returned from the meeting in the Green Circle. They had tried to explain why the Florin Flinging couldn't take place, but the women were having none of it. It was tradition, they had insisted. Besides, they had suffered long enough with no money coming in and having to make do with all other tasks that they shouldn't have to if the quarry was open. They were taking in the laundry for the Lord, threshing the barley for the Lord, churning the butter for the Lord. The women had to fraternise with the Lord, they had argued. Someone had to make a living during the angry time. They were not going to miss out on the many florins they might catch when he did his thing out of the castle window. Today was the day and they were going and that was the end of it!

The women's meeting opened. Sarah held in her right hand the small pink stone she had taken from the box near the lectern in the corner. It glistened in the evening light. She licked the index finger of her right hand and approached Ella, who sat in the rocking chair, book open on her lap, wearing Great Great Old Granny Pink's mountain-shaped hat. Ella was almost invisible to the gathering under that hat. No time for changing your mind and having another go cos you don't like the words, Ella thought to herself under the hat, hoping the reading would be a good one. She read aloud from underneath.

'Draw nigh
To the purple cloth and the split stones
carried over two thresholds.

Pink Granite

Knock the door with both, twice.
Approach the ox in the garden.
And ride.

Ride for your life!'

The room of women shuddered and muttered, 'It's the time. It's the time.'
Ella continued:

'So I left the purple and split rocks with the ox in the garden.
Walking back from whence I had come,
I saw two twigs with roots.
I placed them on my head.
I became a young antlered stag.
I broke the twigs off my head.
I took them to the pile.
There was a smell of burning.
From the burning came a message,

From the taxi rank,
From the bus station,
Through the telephone and the intercom.'

More words like the other day, that Ella and Sarah had never heard of, nor the women
of the village. Strange words from a different time.

'From the space that is outer
And the space that is inner
From the diggers and the starships
Through mechanical things:
Rotators
and
Zoomers
and
Boomers

and
all techie things
Thingamajigs with wings
through the airwaves
Buzzing and whirring
From the Starmen
Legions of them
All calling occupants from 1970.
Save our Souls!
Save our Souls!
Save our Souls!
Amplify the old lady past her sell-by date,
And bring in the big hard energy
factory man!'

With that, a bee buzzed in through the door of the blessing hut even though it was getting dark. And five big black meat flies orbited around the candle on the table near the lectern before ascending to the roof.

There was a loud knock at the door.

'Is there anybody there?'

'Yes, and that person be you, kind friend,' said Jenny Left Foot, Tommy's wife, sitting nearest to the door. She did it just like that – automatically.

In walked Great Great Old Granny Pink.

'Is there anybody there?' called the Dark One.

'Yes, and that person be you, kind friend,' said Great Great Old Granny Pink.

In walked the Dark One with a deep dark look in her eye. She's got eyes in the back of her head, thought each woman, each one knowing the skills and knowledge the Dark One had collected over the years.

47

There was a flash of lightning and a crack of thunder. The window in the far turret flung open. The quarrymen burst through, all squashed inside the window frame, anxious to hear the outcome of the resurrected Granny Pink.

Chapter Eight
Low Tide

Pink Granite

'Imposters! Liars! Sacrilege!' the throng of women hissed at Ella and Sarah.

No sooner had the turret window flung open to reveal the eavesdropping quarrymen than the women had charged back through the wooden door of the blessing hut, pushing past Great Great Old Granny Pink, the Dark One and the desperately confused sisters, who were still clutching the book and the stone. The girls stood there with no congregation except for the two old women and the desperate quarrymen looking despairingly through the turret window.

'We will have our Florin Flinging! You can't stop us!'

Their voices raged into the distance as they made their way to the sandy mudflats that revealed themselves in the moonlight between Core Rock and the island where Sea Stone was sleeping. He had gone to bed early so he would be awake for low tide, when he would fling his florins.

Back at the blessing hut, aghast and bewildered, the men clambered through the windows to comfort their crying children, now abandoned by their mothers. The wailing in the blessing hut was unbearable. Screams and sobs of 'Mammy! Mammy! Mammy! I want my Mammy! Where's my Mammy gone?' filled the hot angry air that consumed the once-so-sacred place.

Great Great Old Granny Pink grabbed her book from Ella, opening it with the speed of one who knows her book well.

'When the Green Circle comes into the holy place,
Woe betide, Woe betide!'

She had taken up her familiar spot again.

Ella and Sarah retreated to the blessing hut kitchen, thinking they should make tea. The Dark One consoled the men through the window, who just didn't know what to do. She urged them to come to the door of the blessing hut and complete the entrance ritual to help make things right again. Those men and young boys who didn't have children rushed round to the door to do just that, but the fathers amongst them were not for playing 'silly games', or so that ritual seemed now. They pushed past the others, determined to console their children. Some even stood on the windowsill and leapt down into the hut, ignoring all the rituals and the rules. Everything seemed to be falling apart to Ella and Sarah, aghast at these sights.

Meanwhile, on the mudflats, the great walk, now a run towards Lord Sea Stone's castle, had begun. The women lifted their long skirts to avoid the lapping tide that was almost fully out.

'It's late,' warned Jenny. 'We've almost missed it. Soon it will be at its lowest point, then the hush, and then the turn,' she urged.

No one took any notice. Everything was going so fast as the women sploshed their way towards the promise from the castle window. To avoid a queue and in the rush, the women made a long line. From a distance it looked like a dark peninsula in the moonlight, long and thin, stretching for miles, it seemed. The line got closer and closer to the castle. Then there was a hush. The tide turned just as the line of women curved in on itself underneath the castle window of bounty. The florins poured out from the open window, plopping into the lapping tide. The women grappled and fought for the florins in the soggy sand, witnessing the bounty slowly sinking into the sand.

The water rose and began to surround the grovelling women, and very quickly their boots became full, their upturned aprons soggy and sagging with florins. The sea ebbed and flowed and ebbed and flowed, threatening to cover them.

'We have to go back now. We won't be able to walk with our heads down low if we don't go back now,' called Jenny as she began the ritual of walking backwards, as was the custom and the tradition.

The angry time had brought great hardship to the women of Core Rock, and they were not going to miss out on these extra florins to make ends meet.

'Come hell or high water!' called the throng.

'Come hell or high water!' echoed around the horseshoed crowd underneath the Lord's windowsill.

The water was getting so high now that some women were floating, doggie paddling on their backs, still holding their aprons flat and floating with the florins. A few with Jenny nearer to Core Rock beach, who hadn't tried to get more florins, had managed to struggle backward, walking with heads bowed low, gasping and gurgling in the water that threatened to take away their last breath. These women lolloped backwards, finally keeling over on their backs, their florins resting like stones on their flattened bellies.

Dawn broke to reveal another line of people on the beach.

The husbands and the fathers and the sons and the men with no children were calling out, 'Come back! Come back! Come back!'

When Jenny and her companions stood up, their backs aching from bending over, they could see the array of the other women's arms flapping about in the sea, calling out, 'Save our souls! Save our souls! Save our souls!'

Some had given up their florins, their need for their dear lives taking hold of them. Desperate, their bodies turned and they lashed the water with their arms and legs, hauling themselves ashore.

Others, determined to keep going, were lost.

Chapter Nine
Jimmy Goes over the Edge

Pink Granite

By the time the sun had fully risen, they were all there – those who hadn't drowned, that is. It was a terrible sight. Tommy Left Foot consoled his wife, Jenny, who consoled the women she had waded back with. They consoled their friends, their lovers and their fathers and whoever else they could.

Jimmy Shanks One Ear, the One Ear you haven't yet met, called out above the crowd:

'Disaster! Disaster!
Jimmy's fell off the edge.
Ring the bell,
Fetch the stretcher.
He's hurt real bad.
Get his mother!'

Like many of the faithful who had studied and learned from the book off by heart, Jimmy Shanks One Ear, cousin to the One Ear family in our tale, was distraught.

'But he can't get his mother,' he wailed.

'But he can't get his mother,' he wailed again.

'But he can't get his mother, for she's deep in the sea and lost forever!' And he fell to the ground, sobbing his poor young heart out.

As is often the case in families, happenings repeat themselves but in different ways.

The survivors joined in the chant, as if to try to pacify him and themselves for many lost loved ones that night. Their tone was low and full of harmony, as if the surrounding mountains were singing their song of honour to Jimmy's ancestor who had lost the land to Lord Sea Stone many years before, before the angry time and before the first mountain was quarried and the accidents had become many.

'The Grand Old Duke had gashed his shin
And ripped his ear off
Marching up and down that hill.

Pink Granite

Up Up
Down Down
Ten thousand of them quarrymen
In a dispute over health and safety.

When Jimmy went over the edge
His pouch went with him.
The gravel went with him.
His snap went with him.
His wages went with him.
And he left his ear halfway up and halfway down.

When a tree with a sticky out leg
Ripped into his shin,
His heart stopped beating for five whole minutes.
In those five whole minutes
Jimmy had a vision.

He saw a woman in black
With a stick,
A pot and a spoon.'

And there they stopped, for they couldn't sing about the throne, for there was no throne for our Jimmy, descendant of the Shanks One Ears of Core Rock. When Lord Sea Stone had come upon these parts, he had taken the land with a trumped-up promise, backed by the Centre Fold, to make the sale pay well for the families there. He had modernised the quarry work, promising an end to their struggles and their accidents. This is how it is with land and property.

Somewhere in the land, often far away from where the land in question is, someone with the power declares how things should be run, and it's as if they are making it up as they go along. Lord Sea Stone had presented the Shanks One Ears, the former land inhabitants, with a piece of paper from the Centre Fold declaring his right intentions, and they just had to take it on the chin.

Pink Granite

There were many One Ear families in those old days who were presented with the paper from the Centre Fold and their land handed over to the Lord.

The singers ended.

'Gash Gash Gash!
Gosh Gosh Gosh!
Gosh Gosh Gosh!'

They knew this family story off by heart. It was written in the book. Great Great Old Granny Pink read it from the book. Often. So often that Ella and Sarah had become bored by it. But today Jimmy Shanks One Ear's accident had repeated itself, calling through the generations in a way not ever dreamed of. The loss was huge and the sorrow even huger.

After the long silence that followed the song, some of the men and boys waded out to sea to search for the bodies of the women who had drowned. Other men and boys waited for bodies to wash up on the shore. The dawn dragged out like a long lament, calling out to the castle on the island to no avail.

It was a pinkish dawn with red hues dappled with yellow. As the colours deepened on the horizon, you could just make out the dark shape of a boat steering its way towards Core Rock's shore. It had come from beyond the castle, it seemed. Looking closer, you could see it was Grand Old Lord Sea Stone standing tall like a mast, his pink coat fluttering, blowing in the breeze and glistening in the morning sun just like in one of the paintings of him. A closer look also revealed a sea chest full of florins. Sitting beside the Old Lord and guarding the chest were Rock Hard and Big Hand, two of the strongest, most muscular men in Core Rock.

This strange, unexpected alliance confused the swimmers searching for their women and the boys and men waiting on the shore.

What are those two doing fraternising with the Lord? thought every survivor of the night's tragic events, but no one said anything to anybody. It was tradition not to question in front of the Lord; it would have to wait for later. It would need to be written down and questioned in the proper way, on paper.

Grand Old Lord Sea Stone had brought along his personal painter. Here was a scene to be witnessed and painted, he had thought when he set off on the journey from the other side of the island, where he kept his fleet of boats. It was the morning after his generous Florin Flinging, and he needed a record. It was in the Lord's interests to be seen to be helping the village folk, despite the angry time. Unaware of the night's tragedy, this morning he was offering a bonus of florins from his chest.

Standing in his boat, he addressed the quarrymen and the remnant of women left from the drowning. He quickly saw what must have happened and altered his bonus speech to a speech of commiseration or something like that.

'Errrr … last night was a terrible accident,' he said, 'caused by a few awkward people who won't take up my offer. Now see what you have done. Many of your women have drowned, and your families have missed out on the yearly offering from my Florin Flinging. You must keep time with the tide. That is the tradition.'

The men elbowed each other and hissed under their breath.

'Uh uh,' the Lord interjected. 'No need to spit at me. I know your gripes. Now, I have another offer to make. See, my boat is full of florins. I'll give these to you if you will sign your young men and women over to me for the wars in the far-flung lands. The Centre Fold has called, and there are pieces of paper to be signed. While these young ones are gone, the older men can have a share of florins from the chest, but the quarry must reopen.'

It looked a hell of a lot of florins, thought Jenny Left Foot. She elbowed Tommy in the ribs. Would they be considered young enough? Jenny wondered. Florins for a war, she pondered.

At that moment, in amongst the mumbled reactions to the offer, two old women standing on a rock on the beach called out, a huge wailing siren scream like gory gulls come to devour the Lord in one big gulp. Two small figures stood beside them, squawking and crowing in a chorus. Ella and Sarah seemed transformed into black ravens as they perched there, shouting from the rocks. All four had left the blessing hut and followed the men to the beach, watching the proceedings with utter desolation and anger.

Pink Granite

'Woe betide,
When the Centre sends its paper.
Woe betide,
When the pen is in the hand.
Woe betide,
When the Green Circle comes into the holy place
And the tree-mother calls her children.
Woe betide!
There will be a great sorrow.
There will be a great lamentation,
When the people are called to a war
When the children are called to a war
For a Florin
For a Florin.'

Then they sang the song of the Great Lamentation, the one used for funerals, with the loudest wail ever heard of, their croaking voices soaring in the morning sky, and all the gulls and sea birds joined in.

'Lalayo lalayo lalayo layo layo
Lalayo lalayo lalayo layo layo
Lalayo lalayo lalayo layo layo
Lalayo lalayo lalayo layo layo.'

Chapter Ten
Paint the Town Red

It was strange. It was as if the blessing hut and the Steeple House had come together as one on the beach, all high and mighty and deep and lowly at the same time. It was as if everything was turning inside out, including the heartache of the remaining quarry folk. Their goodwill was all laid out bedraggled on the beach. The bodies of the women were washing up, and the menfolk confronted their sorrow yet again as they held their children close. They sobbed and sobbed. As if there hadn't been enough dying for one day and night!

How can we go to war when we've got the children to care for? each thought with a heavy heart and in a desperate quandary. You might think it strange that the reason for the war was not a question to be asked. No one asked anything. The angry time had meant you didn't fraternise with the Lord. You didn't speak with him. And you certainly didn't question him. The air was silent and thick with anger.

Lord Sea Stone, oblivious, posed motionless in his boat. His painter carefully worked at her new commissioned painting of him standing generously offering his boat full of florins and wafting his papers in the faces of the quarry folk. He was numb to the excessive demands he had made upon the people of Core Rock. It was ludicrous, and you couldn't make it up.

Sarah, having come closer to the scene with her fellow crowers, thought she knew that painter. She was sure she had seen her working away in one of the rooms in the castle when Great Great Old Granny Pink had taken her over to clean the silver, before the angry time and the time before Great Great Old Granny Pink had become sleepy. Sarah had seen that painter in the shadows flitting about. Who was she?

Breaking through the silent thickness, Tommy Left Foot came forward for the deal on offer, head up, hand held out. Sea Stone rattled the papers impatiently in front of the other men, feeling he had secured a certain bargain with Tommy at least.

'That's it, son. You take the lead. The rest will follow, as is their debt. Paint, Narcissa, paint me. And ensure you include some of the folk in a queue before me. Continue. Vite, vite!' he barked at his painter, whose name we now know is Narcissa.

Pink Granite

Great Great Old Granny Pink, fully recovered through the Dark One's wonderful work, had returned to herself. Standing with her crowing comrades, she saw her chance. She would make the Lord hear the words from her book. They would persuade him against the war, she was sure. So she positioned herself at the end of the jetty where the boats usually moored when they collected the rock to take to foreign parts. This was the nearest spot to Lord Sea Stone's position. She asked her crow companions to hold her book open. She read. She read as if the very stone on which she had stood earlier was crying out above the waves that washed ashore:

'From the space that is outer
And the space that is inner
From the diggers and the starships
Through
Mechanical things:
Rotators
and
Zoomers
and
Boomers
and
all things techie like
Thingamajigs with wings
through the airwaves
Buzzing and whirring
From the Starmen
Legions of them
All calling occupants from 1970.
Save our Souls!
Save our Souls!
Save our Souls!
Amplify the old lady past her sell-by date,
And bring in the big hard energy
factory man!'

Pink Granite

But Narcissa couldn't paint. She had frozen solid with her red-loaded brush dripping scarlet blobs on the sandy shore. She stopped her work, gazing at Great Great Old Granny Pink. As if in a trance, and with an expression of recognition, she joined in with the reader. But she didn't need to read, for the words just flowed out from her heart:

'Over the cliff edge
The cliff is crumbling
Rock
Pink rock
Like rhubarb
Like giant rhubarb leaves
Rhubarb and custard
Umbrella leaves
Custard skin
And jug ear leaves
Seaside leaves
Ice cream milk and dairy cow leaves
Dairy farmer fishwife
Fisher
Fiskmann
Pescetarianman
Vegan Man
Vegetarian
Carcass
Meat chop
Dig and cut.
Dig and cut.

In the granite quarry of your grandfathers at Stoney Stanton,
Bedworth
and Coverntree,
In Richard's Red Leicester out at Broughton Astley
Blasting the ship foghorns bound for
Canada, Brownsburg and Quebec

Pink Granite

> A baby, a wife and on
> Through the Great War
> Ride the Horse that is Teuton
> Then come back again.'

'Pull yourself together, woman, and paint me!' thundered Lord Sea Stone, rocking his boat, nearly losing his balance. The Dark One, holding a bowl of earth with yellow trumpet-shaped flowers with orange centres, walked slowly forward along the jetty. Tommy still stood, his hand outstretched to receive his call-up papers.

'Tommy, behold your dad. Tommy, behold your mam,' the Dark One declared, tipping the earth and its yellow flowers over Tommy's head like some kind of strange baptism.

All at once a gust of wind swept the papers from Sea Stone's grasp and he keeled over.

The crowd hushed, and the men clutched their children even more tightly for fear the same might happen to them.

Those women who had survived approached the boat, their hearts and voices raging with all the anthems ever heard of in every language imaginable. The babble was like rumbling thunder echoing along the beach and up to the mountain. Lightning struck, and it was as if the whole mountain cracked open. Out of the mountain's summit, a naked umbrella-shaped thing sizzled and sparked. Speaking with a metallic voice, the skeletal umbrella joined the raging women:

> 'Thou art our Tommy's Daddy and we all know it's true
> All glory laud and honour and that's the end of you.'

Ella, as we know, loved the book and its strange utterings, so she secretly offered an explanation about the umbrella and the sparky thing coming out of the top of the mountain. The revelation was jaw-dropping information for the remaining people of Core Rock. One of their own sired by the Grand Old Lord and an umbrella thingy poking out of the top of the mountain. How did that happen?

Pink Granite

'No, absolutely not!' screamed Grand Old Lord Sea Stone, his face getting redder and redder.

'Yes, absolutely so, Daddy,' cried Tommy, stretching his arms in the direction of Narcissa and his newly proclaimed father. The florin had dropped.

'And the Lord, wearing his pink stone-coloured garment,
carrying his pink and black spotted umbrella
stole into the room where the woman of the yellow flower lay.'

The truth was out. Sea Stone raged back, sticking his fingers in both ears and singing his own melody at the top of his voice:

'Ariolg
ell nyer devyer filiasum
E remi ny demi lo la thida swello
Nielf sa za ziwani sverso schnoosi
Niet na var nor vieig vergauche nyei.'

'It must be Latin,' whispered Sarah to Ella, for Ella could not translate that babble. It couldn't have been from the book.

'My final offer to clear all this up is the chance to serve your people in the war abroad. The offer is on the table,' declared the Lord, finally pulling himself together.

Great Great Old Granny Pink continued with her book.

'When the Lord calls for the soldier,
And the dead are not yet buried,
Who will plough the fields?
Who will plant the furrows?

In the granite quarry of your grandfathers at Stoney Stanton,
Bedworth
and Coverntree,

Pink Granite

In Richard's Red Leicester out at Broughton Astley
Blasting the ship foghorns bound for
Canada, Brownsburg and Quebec
A baby, a wife and on
Through the Great War
Ride the Horse that is Teuton
Then come back again.'

And all the people chorused:
'We won't come back again.
We won't come back again.
We won't come back again.'

They had decided. They formed a long, meandering line processing from the beach
back to the blessing hut, for they would rather bury their dead than serve their lord
and master and his wars in foreign parts a moment longer.

'Paint, Narcissa, paint!' he cried, all alone in his boat, up to his neck in florins.

But Narcissa, along with her son Tommy, his wife Jenny and the others, were way at
the front of the procession carrying their next-door neighbour's body, as so many
of the Core Rock folk did that day. They all walked the long stony pathway from
the beach to the village and on to the blessing hut, their voices ringing out, echoing
across the half-eaten mountains. The Dark One, Great Great Old Granny Pink, Great
Old White Beard, Brother Will, Sarah and Ella walked at the rear, with Jimmy Shanks
following in the far distance, his coat flapping in the wind. There were another two
years like this, for it became known as the long angry time.

Epilogue

Daff and Redhair gently closed the book as the chief city archivist called time for the day.

'I think I'm a Sea Stone,' Daff said, putting her gloved hand to her mouth.

'And I think I'm a One Ear,' gasped Redhair.

ACKNOWLEDGEMENTS
Catherine Dunn, Joanna Moxham, David Oswald, Robert Oswald, Nia Phillips, Richard Talbot and The Project Group, Dorset 2022/23: Sian Alcock, Rachel Ballin, Paul Baxter, Mary Booker, Andrew Carey, Caroline Hepworth, Natalie Lee, Sandra Reeve, Simon Slidders, Beate Stuehm, Penny Stirling, Paule Yeomans.

ABOUT THE AUTHOR
Carran Waterfield is an international award-winning theatre and performance maker, writer and creative teacher. She has produced a body of devised professional works spanning over thirty years. She is the Artistic Director and Founder of award-winning Triangle Theatre est. 1988 (Coventry, UK). She is a practising performance artist and author. She is also a published poet and playwright. She was born in Coventry, where for many years she lived, taught and made her theatre and performance work. She moved to Southport, Merseyside (UK) in 2010.
www.carranwaterfield.co.uk
instagram.com/carranwaterfield

ABOUT THE ILLUSTRATOR
Fruzsina Czech is an award-winning illustrator, storyteller, pencil collector and creative person. Her work communicates stories through figurative illustration full of character, inspired by a mix of observation, memories and imagination, mainly focusing her work on publishing and commercial illustration at the moment.
She recently relocated to Budapest to play scrabble with her Granny on Wednesdays.
www.fruzic.com
instagram.com/fruzic